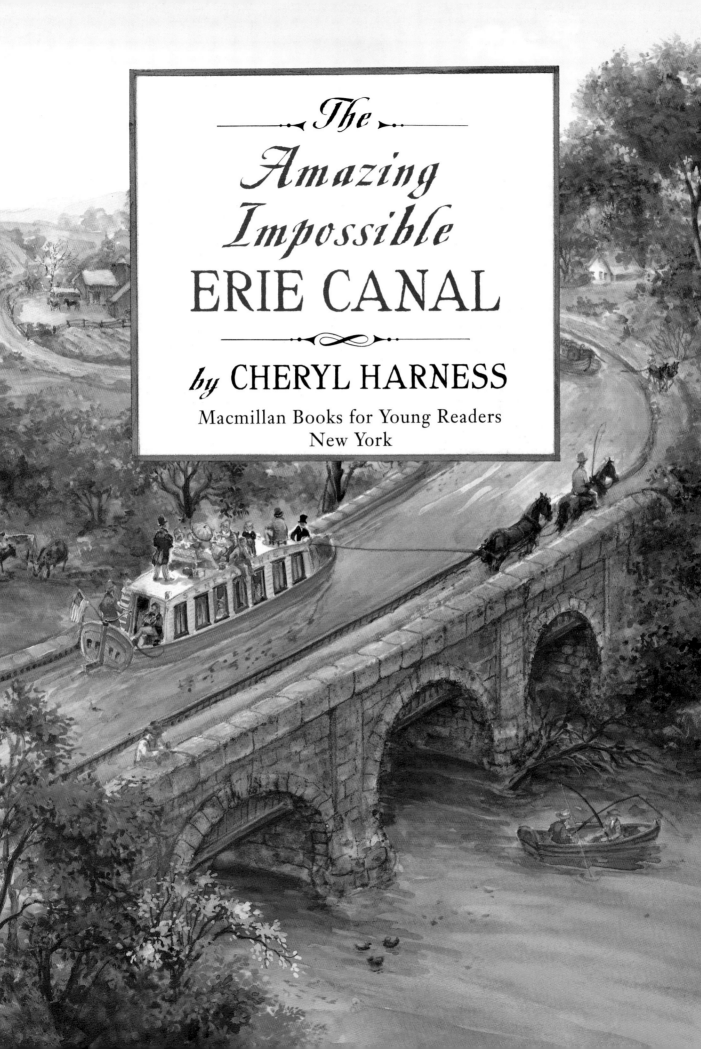

The
Amazing
Impossible
ERIE CANAL

by CHERYL HARNESS

Macmillan Books for Young Readers
New York

ACKNOWLEDGEMENTS

I wish to acknowledge the assistance of Professor Frederick J. Blue, Youngstown State University, who helped keep the facts straight; the inspiring work of the staff at Erie Canal Village at Rome, New York; Sheryl Woods of New York's Division of Tourism; and, as always, I wish to thank Barbara Lalicki, who edited this book.

MACMILLAN BOOKS FOR YOUNG READERS
An imprint of Simon & Schuster Children's Publishing Division
1230 Avenue of the Americas
New York, New York 10020

The text of this book is set in 14 pt. Janson.
The illustrations were done in watercolor, gouache, and colored pencil.
The music copyist is Christina Davidson.
Printed and bound in Hong Kong by South China Printing Company
(1988) Ltd. on chlorine-free, acid-free paper.
First edition

10 9 8 7 6 5 4 3 2 1

LIBRARY OF CONGRESS CATALOGING-IN-PUBLICATION DATA
Harness, Cheryl.
The amazing impossible Erie Canal / by Cheryl Harness. — 1st ed.
p.   cm.
Includes bibliographical references.
ISBN 0-02-742641-6
1. Erie Canal (N.Y.)—History—Juvenile literature.   [1. Erie Canal (N.Y.)—History.]   I. Title.
F127.E5H37   1995
977.1'2—dc20   94-11114

Summary: The conception and building of the Erie Canal, the ten-day parade down the canal led by the *Seneca Chief*, and the effects of the canal on the developing nation.

This book is for Raymond, my dad;
Kim, my friend;
and Mary Beth, my hero.

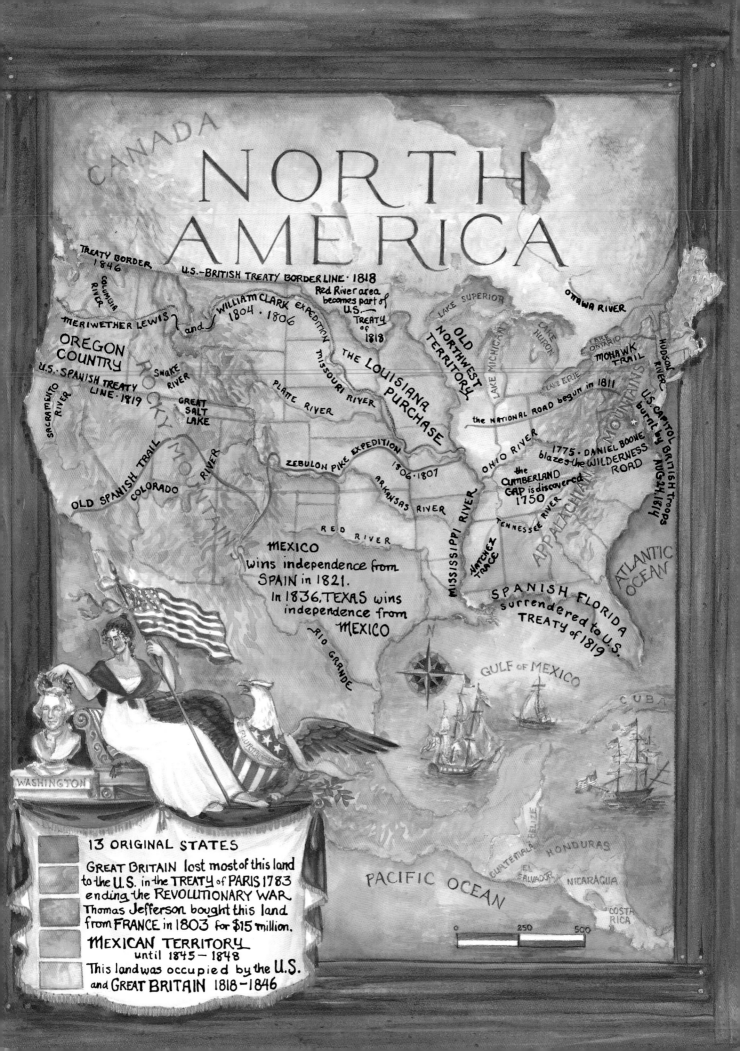

After a second war against Great Britain, the War of 1812, the people of the United States were feeling confident about the future of their expanding nation. Thousands of pioneers struggled over a rough barrier: the thickly wooded Appalachian Mountains that extended down the continent. On the other side was the tantalizing West, stretching clear to the Mississippi River and beyond.

Settlers' wagons jolted miserably down roads that once had been Indian trails. When farmers and fur trappers got to the lonely frontier, they found that it cost too much and took too long to ship apples, flour, wood, and pelts to the eastern markets. Eastern merchants had no easy way to sell axes, plows, and buttons to customers in the West.

CATARAQUI

LAKE ONTARIO

LAKE GEORGE

From Fort Stanwix (ROME) boats were carried 2 miles to WOOD CREEK which flowed into ONEIDA LAKE

OSWEGO FALLS

ONEIDA LAKE

FORT STANWIX

NIAGARA FALLS

TONAWANDA CREEK

GENESEE RIVER

ONANDAGA RIVER

WOOD CREEK

MOHAWK RIVER

SCHENECTADY

BUFFALO on the shore of LAKE ERIE

marshes and swamps

LITTLE FALLS

OKSWEGO

KEUKA LAKE

SENECA LAKE

CAYUGA LAKE

10   20   30 miles

SCHOHARIE CREEK

Boats had to be carried for a mile around the rapids at LITTLE FALLS.

Dutch colonists founded their settlement here in 1624. They called it FORT ORANGE. Later, it would be called ALBANY

Henry HUDSON explored this river in 1609.

It took nearly a month or more to get a barrel of flour from the shores of Lake Erie along the Mohawk Trail to the Hudson River. However difficult, this passage followed a natural gap in the Appalachian range. Since ancient times, native peoples such as the Senecas and Onandagas had floated their light canoes along the Mohawk River, Wood Creek, and Oneida Lake on the way to Lakes Ontario and Erie. They carried the canoes around the rapids, over land, and through valleys where boats couldn't go.

European colonists moved their heavy, flat-bottomed boats on the same waterways. They, too, had to work around the obstructions. Why not connect these rivers and lakes with man-made streams, as in the Old Country? they wondered. Smoothly floating boats could be pulled along by horses walking on the bank. After the War of Independence was over in 1783, George Washington himself championed the idea of such canals: Travel and trade made easy and cheap would hold a young country together. If such a waterway was constructed between the Great Lakes and the Hudson, a person could float from Ohio clear to London! It seemed an impossible dream.

If only the millions of dollars could be raised . . . if only all the engineering problems could be solved . . . a ditch 40 feet wide carrying 4 feet of water could be made to go up and down 363 miles across the countryside. . . . *Impossible!*

Nevertheless, a politician named De Witt Clinton argued that the canal was more than possible, it was necessary; not only for New York but for America. It would be a pathway into the country's heartland. The people agreed, and Mr. Clinton became the governor.

On a long-awaited summer morning, gentlemen wearing tall silk hats gathered in a meadow near Rome, New York, in the level center of the state, where the digging was easy. Romans wore their best clothes, and a band played a fanfare on shiny cornets as the ground was broken for the Erie Canal at dawn on the Fourth of July, 1817.

How the CANAL was built 1817~1825

LAKE ONTARIO

Brilliant Nathan Roberts engineered the "Lockport Five," the only 2-way locks on the CANAL. They climbed the NIAGARA ESCARPMENT

After 2 years of blasting and building the LOCKPORT LOCKS were finished JUNE 24, 1825

OCTOBER 1823 The canal is open between BROCKPORT and ALBANY 275 miles

OCTOBER 1822 The ERIE CANAL is completed from ROCHESTER to LITTLE FALLS 180 miles

NIAGARA FALLS

GASPORT MEDINA ALBION
LOCKPORT
PENDLETON

ROCHESTER
BROCKPORT

The CANAL was dug in both directions at once.

FAIRPORT
PALMYRA LYONS
THE ERIE CANAL
MONTEZUMA

GRAND ISLAND
TONAWANDA
BLACK ROCK
BUFFALO THE ERIE CANAL was finished here OCTOBER 1825

Benjamin Wright chief engineer of the MIDDLE SECTION

James Geddes explored western New York in 1808 looking for the best course for the Canal.

malaria killed hundreds of diggers in the MONTEZUMA MARSHES

LAKE ERIE

Thousands of trees had to be gotten out of the way of the CANAL. This huge machine was invented to pull up the stumps. When a team of mules pulled the ropes around the center wheel, the chain around the mighty axle yanked out even the most stubborn stumps.

Governor Clinton sent young **Canvass White** to study the English canals, especially their LOCKS.

He brought back hundreds of drawings.

How LOCKS work

① the boat enters the lock through one of the MAIN GATES

②

③

④

MAIN GATE
SLUICE GATE
BALANCE BEAM

As water flows in (or out) the SLUICE GATE, the boat is raised (or lowered) to the next level.

90 feet long
15 feet wide

BRIDGES THAT CARRY WATER
18 AQUEDUCTS were built to carry the CANAL over rivers and valleys.

• 83 LOCKS • were built to carry the CANAL over the shape of the land. They were built with carefully cut stone blocks held together with the waterproof cement invented by Canvass White.

After the ground breaking at ROME, JULY 4, 1817, then came the stake-setters, the soil-borers, the underbrush-grubbers, the tree-chopper-downers, stump-pullers, and root-cutters, ditch-diggers and dirt-movers. Hundreds of workers came from hungry IRELAND. They overcame their fears of American wildcats, owls, and snakes. Hard workers dug in and created the

ERIE CANAL

363 miles long, the longest uninterrupted canal in the world.

OSWEGO

The MIDDLE SECTION 94 miles from MONTEZUMA to UTICA opened for business JULY 4, 1820.

ONEIDA LAKE

WOOD CREEK

ROME

ORISKANY

UTICA

LITTLE FALLS

MOHAWK RIVER

WEEDSPORT

SYRACUSE

ONEIDA

the 15 miles between ROME and UTICA were the first completed OCTOBER 1819

HERKIMER

scale of miles
0 5 10

0 5 10 15
km

N
S

Bridges were built low to save money.

SCHENECTADY is 218 feet higher than ALBANY 2 AQUEDUCTS and 27 LOCKS stair-stepped to the HUDSON RIVER

This bank is the BERM

The TOW PATH is 10 feet wide

——— 40 feet wide at the surface ———
4 feet deep
——— 28 feet wide at the bottom ———

Five years later, the people were worried the project would never be paid for or finished. The governor lost his job. Mr. Clinton kept overseeing the work and making speeches anyway. His political enemies called the canal Clinton's Ditch.

But the voters felt better as they traveled more and more on the almost-finished waterway, which was already earning money in tolls. (For example, one penny for one ton of grain hauled one mile.) Mr. Clinton won the election of 1824. The following year, the impossible Erie Canal was done; *Clinton's Ditch* was said with pride. It was time to celebrate.

TEN O'CLOCK WEDNESDAY MORNING
OCTOBER 26, 1825

BOOM! the Buffalo cannon thundered.

It was echoed by a distant THOOMP from Black Rock, to the north. Birds fluttered up in clouds from the bright fall treetops. Gun by gun, from Lake Erie, 363 miles down the amazing ribbon of water, and down the Hudson River to the sea, the news was signaled: After eight years of work, the Erie Canal was done.

Four gray horses headed down the towpath pulling the *Seneca Chief*, Governor De Witt Clinton's packet. The *Seneca Chief* was followed by four more packets, as the sleek horse-drawn passenger boats were called. Loud were the cheers from the crowd and the music from the band, and louder still were the rifle salutes fired into the sky. Besides people, the *Seneca Chief* carried green painted kegs of water from Lake Erie for the ceremony at the end of the journey. Lake water poured into the salty Atlantic Ocean would mean that the waters of East and West were connected at last.

The water current pushed the Eastbound boats through the locks on the left.

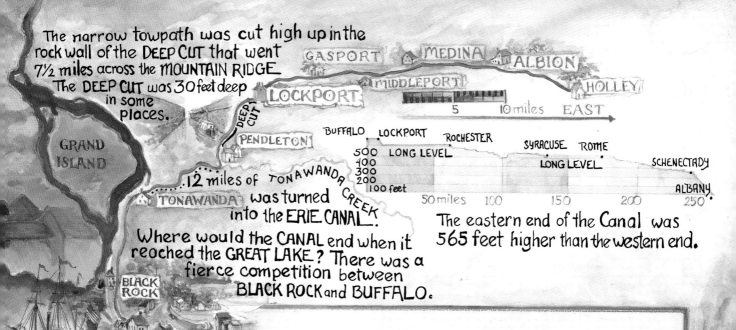

The narrow towpath was cut high up in the rock wall of the DEEP CUT that went 7½ miles across the MOUNTAIN RIDGE. The DEEP CUT was 30 feet deep in some places.

GASPORT   MEDINA   ALBION
MIDDLEPORT   HOLLEY
LOCKPORT
                    5   10 miles   EAST

GRAND ISLAND

DEEP CUT
PENDLETON

BUFFALO LOCKPORT   ROCHESTER   SYRACUSE ROME   SCHENECTADY
500 LONG LEVEL   LONG LEVEL
400
300
200
100 feet   50 miles   100   150   200   250
                                                        ALBANY

12 miles of TONAWANDA CREEK was turned into the ERIE CANAL.

TONAWANDA

The eastern end of the Canal was 565 feet higher than the western end.

Where would the CANAL end when it reached the GREAT LAKE? There was a fierce competition between BLACK ROCK and BUFFALO.

BLACK ROCK

BUFFALO

The gaily decorated horses *clop-clopped* at four miles an hour. Every ten miles or so, fresh teams of horses or mules replaced the tired animals on the towing ropes. More canal boats joined the procession in Lockport. They were all floated sixty-three feet down the five double-stair–step locks, already famous as great feats of engineering. The locks were built into a massive ridge of limestone, the toughest obstacle in the path of the canal.

The people on the packets stared, full of wondering, at the fitted stones in the wet walls as the gates were opened and closed, allowing water to flow out to the next lock, lowering boats one by one, level by level.

"Amazing!"

After feasting, fireworks, and speeches at Lockport, the parade of boats continued east, past bonfires on the bluffs and cabins with candles burning in every window. Late into the October night, the governor stood with the captain at the tiller watching bats and moths dance in the lantern light. The towropes made shimmers on the dark water. Clinton thought of the long years of hot debates and hard digging, then he savored the sounds of cowbells, bullfrogs, and steady hoofbeats on the towpath.

LAKE ONTARIO

HOLLEY ADAMS BASIN

BROCKPORT SPENCERPORT

ROCHESTER 2 to 7:30 p.m.

The boats were greeted at HOLLEY early in the morning of Thursday, October 27 the 2nd day

FAIRPORT
PITTSFORD

CLINTON and the CANAL

MACEDON

the 3rd day

breakfast in PALMYRA Friday October 28

LYONS CLYDE

PALMYRA

PORT GIBSON   NEWARK 11 a.m.

2 to 4 p.m.

10:30 p.m.

MONTEZUMA fireworks!

A mighty aqueduct 802 ft. long spanned the GENESEE RIVER. Here, the ROCHESTER packet, YOUNG LION of the WEST joined the procession. Less than 20 years later, this aqueduct was replaced with one with 2 lanes and no leaks.

SENECA CH

The people of PORT BYRON launched an illuminated balloon: High on a hill over the village, a bonfire blazed to welcome the boats from the WEST.

ONEIDA LAKE

Sunday morning October 30 ROME

VERONA

ONEIDA

PORT BYRON   JORDAN   4th day of the voyage

SYRACUSE 2 p.m. October 29 in time for dinner

LENOX

SULLIVAN

CHITTENANGO

5   10 miles

WEEDSPORT

Two young men of WEEDSPORT were killed when the celebration cannon went off by accident.

MANLIUS

In the rainy afternoon of the second day, the growing procession of boats reached Rochester, nearly ninety-three miles out from Buffalo. The next morning, the boats passed under an arch at Macedon where a banner hailed CLINTON AND THE CANAL. With bellies full of breakfast, ears full of patriotic speeches, on the passengers went.

"Bridge!" called the driver boys up ahead.

"Low bridge!" Puffing, grumbling, and laughing, the ladies and gentlemen ducked down low as the farmers and villagers on the bridge shouted, "Hurrah!"

The 29th of October marked the fourth day of the great journey to the East. The boats were towed to Syracuse for a celebration supper.

Sunday morning, on the fifth day, the *Seneca Chief* was greeted by the villagers of Rome. It was here that the digging had begun eight long years before. Between Rome and Utica, fifteen miles east, the Erie Canal had been open since 1819, but, to the Romans' sorrow, the main waterway ended up bypassing the center of their village, where only a bit of old canal remained. Some put aside their hurt feelings to cheer the governor and the packets from the West.

October 31, the 6th day
The boats leave UTICA
8 a.m. Monday

November 1.
the 7th day

ROME

THE MOHAWK RIVER

ORISKANY

LITTLE FALLS

HERKIMER

Journey in the
dead of night

5   10 miles

FONDA

AMSTERDAM

The 5th
day

UTICA
12:30 p.m. FRANKFORT
The travelers
go to church and stay for
supper and speeches.

ILION

THE ERIE CANAL

FORT
PLAIN

CANAJOHARIE

NELLISTON

PALITINE
BRIDGE

SPRAKERS

RANDALL

FULTONVILLE

ROTTERDAM

"Congratulations, Governor," shouted the pathmaster, "and to your lady!"

Mr. Clinton tipped his tall hat as his wife nodded her silk bonnet. The pathmaster's job was to keep cows, pigs, fishermen, and buggy races off the towpath. He carried a bundle of straw on his back for plugging leaks made by pesky minks and muskrats tunneling in the banks. If a canal bank gave way, farmers' fields could be flooded, leaving a muddy ditch and stranded boats.

The night of the sixth day was Halloween. Bonfires burned high on the crags and cliffs at Little Falls, where the wild Mohawk River foamed and crashed 30 feet below the triple-arched aqueduct that carried the canal eastward. The procession floated 94 feet downward through 13 locks along the 40 miles to Schenectady. Inside the boats the next morning, the people could hear cold November rain on the roof. The steersmen at the tillers pulled their collars high about their ears. The horses on the towpath lowered their heads.

Twenty-six more stone and timber locks carried them 218 feet deeper down the last 30 miles of the river valley into the sunny morning of November 2, 1825. It had taken just seven days to go from Buffalo to Albany, where the Erie Canal emptied into the Hudson River.

REXFORD
WATER-
FORDA
SCHENECTADY
ALBANY
10:30am.
the 8th
day
HUDSON RIVER

Thousands of people lined the canal banks, towpath, and berm. Brass bands, schoolchildren, and veterans of the War of 1812 waited with old soldiers of the Revolution who'd polished their medals and muskets.

Some folks dressed in Dutch colonial costumes they'd found in their pointy attics.

Cannon fire vibrated the air. "Here they come!"

Governor Clinton stepped down off the *Seneca Chief* to preside over a pageant of lofty words and entertainments. Banners read PEACE AND COMMERCE and THE GRAND WORK IS DONE.

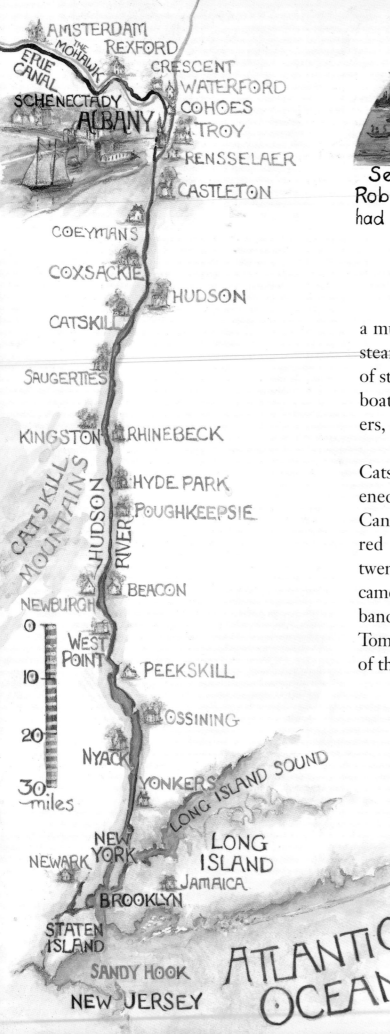

AMSTERDAM
THE
MOHAWK REXFORD
ERIE CRESCENT
CANAL WATERFORD
SCHENECTADY COHOES
ALBANY TROY
RENSSELAER
CASTLETON
COEYMANS
COXSACKIE
HUDSON
CATSKILL
SAUGERTIES
KINGSTON RHINEBECK
CATSKILL MOUNTAINS
HUDSON RIVER
HYDE PARK
POUGHKEEPSIE
BEACON
NEWBURGH
0
WEST POINT
PEEKSKILL
10
OSSINING
20
NYACK
YONKERS
30 LONG ISLAND SOUND
miles
NEW LONG
YORK ISLAND
NEWARK JAMAICA
BROOKLYN
STATEN ISLAND
SANDY HOOK
NEW JERSEY

ATLANTIC OCEAN

Seventeen years earlier, in 1808,
Robert Fulton's little steamboat CLERMONT
had chugged up the HUDSON all by herself.

November 3. This bright autumn day, a multitude gathered to see a fleet of eight steamships shooting sparks, white columns of steam, and black plumes of smoke. Canal boats, all decked out with flags and streamers, set off down the wide river.

The fleet glided past the red-gold Catskill Mountains. When twilight deepened on the river, lanterns were lighted. Cannons thudded, rockets exploded, and red fires burned on the shores. After a twenty-four–gun salute, West Point officers came aboard the *Seneca Chief* for a midnight band concert. Then everyone went to bed. Tomorrow would be a big day: the Wedding of the Waters.

Bells were ringing in the towers and steeples of New York City, where more flag- and bunting-covered steam vessels, barges, and pilot boats joined the fleet. The flotilla sailed past Brooklyn, through the Narrows, down to Sandy Hook on the eastern tip of New Jersey. Here at last, De Witt Clinton lifted a green-and-gold cask to his shoulder and slowly poured water from Lake Erie into the unusually calm and glassy Atlantic Ocean. The mixing together of these waters, fresh and salty, western and eastern, represented a huge accomplishment for a young nation.

Gold medals, souvenirs of the day, would be sent to President John Quincy Adams, his father, John Adams, and the other former presidents still living: Mr. Jefferson, Mr. Madison, and Mr. Monroe.

After the solemn ceremony, musicians aboard two British vessels outside the harbor struck up "Yankee Doodle" in honor of the occasion. The Americans answered with "God Save the King." More salutes were fired, then everybody ate breakfast as they sailed back to the city to watch five thousand marchers in a festive street parade.

Late that night, when the smoke from the fireworks still hung in the air, folks made their ways home through the dark streets, still talking excitedly.

"We'll never see the like of that again—did you see them balls o' fire leapin' out of the roof of City Hall? Rockets, red dragons, and stars rainin' down, by golly!"

"What did that one feller say? . . . 'The longest canal in the world'?"

"That's a fact: the longest in the least time with the least experience and know-how for the least money—"

"Seven millions o' dollars is 'the least money,' you say?"

"Why, price of shipping will drop like an anvil off a roof! Folks going back and forth—in one-third the time! As smooth as you please. . . . Say, there's a ride I'd like to take a whirl at myself . . . ol' Erie Canal."

The *Seneca Chief* returned to Buffalo with a barrel of seawater. Curious day-trippers, New Englanders with "Ohio Fever," immigrants, such foreign travelers as Charles Dickens and the Marquis de Lafayette, as well as families who lived and worked on and about the Erie Canal, all traveled America's first superhighway. The Grand Western Erie Canal had cost $7,143,789 to build. By 1883, the canal would earn seventeen times that amount ($121,461,871 in total revenues).

Many different kinds of boats were seen on the Canal. Bullhead freighters carried flour and grain. LINE BOATS carried both people and freight. They often had a stable in the forward end for the spare team. Square-cornered SCOWS carried lumber and ICE BREAKERS were used to lengthen the boating season.

But the sleek, brightly painted PACKET BOATS were the streamlined queens of the old ERIE CANAL. They carried passengers only, as many as 100 at a time. 80 by 14 feet was the common size of the packets.

The Captain and the Helmsman took turns at the tiller.

After dinner in the main cabin, narrow beds were folded down like "hanging bookshelves".

A curtain separated the ladies' quarters.

Life in the wilderness was transformed by floating libraries, taverns, showboats, and church boats. With flour, beef, wool, and lumber going East, and boatloads of merchandise and settlers going West on the Big Ditch, new towns began and old towns, especially New York City, got bigger and richer. Most of all, the Grand Western Canal, as it was called, was a source of pride for the nation and a link between the old and new states of the Union.

In 1831, a steam locomotive began running on a railway between Albany and Schenectady. As time went by, people wanted to go faster, so they bought railroad tickets, leaving the canal to log rafts, freight boats, and barges. Because of traffic jams, the canal was made wider and deeper, with more double locks for more boats by 1862. By 1918, the Erie Canal had become part of the huge New York State Barge Canal System. It, along with U.S. Interstate 90, follows the ancient Mohawk Trail. De Witt Clinton's once impossible ditch has been bypassed and paved over, locks left to crumble.

New ways have taken its place.

BIBLIOGRAPHY

*Adams, Samuel Hopkins. *The Erie Canal.* New York: Random House, 1953.

*Andrist, Ralph K. *The Erie Canal.* Mahwah, N.J.: Troll Associates, 1964.

Colden, Cadwallader. *Memoir, Prepared at the Request of a Committee of the Common Council of the City of New York and Presented to the Mayor of the City, at the Celebration of the Completion of the New York Canals.* New York: 1825.

Condon, George E. *Stars in the Water.* New York: Doubleday, 1974.

Garrity, Richard. *Canal Boatman.* Syracuse, N.Y.: Syracuse University Press, 1977.

Shaw, Ronald E. *Erie Water West.* Lexington: University of Kentucky Press, 1966.

*Spier, Peter. *The Erie Canal.* New York: Doubleday, 1970.

Wyld, Lionel D. *Low Bridge!* Syracuse, N.Y.: Syracuse University Press, 1962.

Books written especially for young readers